Ash to the Rescue

Adapted by Tracey West

Scholastic Inc.

Poké Rap!

I want to be the very best there ever was
To beat all the rest, yeah, that's my cause

Catch 'em, Catch 'em, Gotta catch 'em all

Pokémon I'll search across the land
Look far and wide
Release from my hand
The power that's inside

Catch 'em, Catch 'em, Gotta catch 'em all Pokémon!

Gotta catch 'em all, Gotta catch 'em all
Gotta catch 'em all, Gotta catch 'em all

At least one hundred and fifty or more to see
To be a Pokémon Master is my destiny

Catch 'em, Catch 'em, Gotta catch 'em all
Gotta catch 'em all, Pokémon! (repeat three times)

Can YOU Rap all 150?

Here's the next 32 Pokémon.
Catch the next book *Secrets of the GS Ball*
for more of the Poké Rap.

Zubat, Primeape, Meowth, Onix
Geodude, Rapidash, Magneton, Snorlax
Gengar, Tangela, Goldeen, Spearow
Weezing, Seel, Gyarados, Slowbro.

Kabuto, Persian, Paras, Horsea
Raticate, Magnemite, Kadabra, Weepinbell
Ditto, Cloyster, Caterpie, Sandshrew
Bulbasaur, Charmander, Golem, Pikachu

Words and Music by Tamara Loeffler and John Siegler
Copyright © 1999 Pikachu Music (BMI)
Worldwide rights for Pikachu Music administered by Cherry River Music Co. (BMI)
All Rights Reserved   Used by Permission

Collect them all!

Ash to the Rescue

© 2018 The Pokémon Company International. © 1997–2018 Nintendo, Creatures, GAME FREAK, TV Tokyo, ShoPro, JR Kikaku. TM, ® Nintendo.

ISBN 978-1-338-28411-9

10 9 8 7 6 5 4 3 2   18 19 20 21 22

Printed in the U.S.A.   40
First printing 2018

Let's Go, Ledyba!

It was a beautiful day in the Johto Region. The sun was shining. The Pidgey were singing.

And Team Rocket was up to no good.

The trio of Pokémon thieves had cut a trapdoor into the walkway of a wooden bridge. Then they tied a large metal cage underneath the trapdoor. Jessie, James, and the Scratch Cat Pokémon, Meowth, stood on top of the cage. They were waiting to set their latest scheme in motion.

Meowth peered through a periscope.

"Ash, Pikachu, and those twerps are headed straight this way," said Meowth.

Jessie chuckled. "Little do they know that their travel plans are about to fall through," she said.

"*Fall through* is right," said James.

"When those twerps get right overhead . . ." Jessie began.

". . . when they're just in the right position . . . " James continued.

". . . we pull the rope, the bottom drops out, and they tumble into the cage," Meowth said gleefully. "Then we slip on the lid, and we got 'em right where we want 'em!'

Jessie got a gleam in her steely blue eyes. "And then Pikachu will be ours!"

Team Rocket was always trying to steal Pikachu, Ash's yellow Electric-type Pokémon. They began to dance and sing at the thought of their impending victory.

"We're gonna catch a Pikachu, we're gonna catch a Pikachu," they chanted, dancing on top of the cage. "We're gonna catch a Pika-huh?"

The wooden boards above them creaked. The cage swung back and forth.

"It's collapsing!" Jessie said.

"So is our plan!" added James.

With a sickening splinter, the boards above them gave way. Jessie, James, Meowth, and the cage splashed into the river below.

"Looks like Team Rocket's splashing off again!" they cried.

Further down the road, Ash Ketchum and his friends made their way toward the bridge. Ash, a Pokémon Trainer, had been busy ever since he came to the Johto Region. His mentor, Professor Oak, had sent him there with a mysterious Poké Ball, the GS Ball. The professor knew of an expert in the Johto Region who might be able to figure out what was inside the GS Ball.

While he was in the Johto Region, Ash was always on the lookout for new Pokémon to capture and train. He also hoped to battle other Trainers at the Johto League gyms. That way, he could earn gym badges, and maybe even a Johto League championship.

Ash wasn't alone on his quest. The Poké Balls he kept in his pockets contained some of his very best Pokémon. Pikachu, a little yellow Pokémon with pointy ears and a lightning bolt-shaped tail, always walked by his side.

His friends Misty and Brock were traveling with him, too. Orange-haired Misty was once a gym leader in Cerulean City. Brock used to be a gym leader, too. Both Brock and Misty had their own Pokémon. They were also kept in Poké Balls, except for Togepi, a Spike Ball Pokémon. Misty carried the tiny Pokémon in her arms.

Together, Ash and his friends were ready for anything.

Except the broken bridge.

Ash walked as far as he could and peered down. The river underneath looked deep — too deep to wade across.

"How are we going to get to the other side?" Ash wondered.

"I guess we could keep walking along the river until we find another bridge," Misty suggested.

Brock's dark hair stuck out above the map he was reading. "According to this, the nearest bridge is ten miles away."

Ash groaned. "There's got to be some other way."

The sound of a shrill whistle interrupted him. It came from above. Ash looked up.

Something was flying above the river. A *lot* of some-things. Ash couldn't quite make out what they were.

As they got closer, Ash saw that he was looking at a group of Bug-type Pokémon. The Pokémon had round,

red bodies. They each had six legs with tiny white feet, and red wings with black circle markings.

A rope was tied to each Pokémon. The ropes were attached to a swing that dangled beneath the Pokémon. A girl with short brown hair sat in the swing. She held a silver whistle in her hand.

"Wow!" Ash remarked. "Let's see what kind of Pokémon they are."

Ash took out Dexter, his Pokédex. The handheld computer had information about all kinds of Pokémon.

Ledyba, the Five Star Pokémon," said Dexter. "These naturally gentle Bug- and Flying-types gather in groups during cold weather to keep warm."

"Bug-type Pokémon usually give me the creeps," Misty admitted, "but these little guys are cute."

The Ledyba and the girl landed on the grass next to them. Brock rushed to greet the girl.

"Thank goodness you've come to save us," Brock gushed. "You're just like an angel from out of the blue."

"My name's Arielle," said the girl. "Can I help you with something?"

"You sure can. We need to get across the river," Ash said. He nudged his friend, who was still staring at Ariel with lovesick eyes. "And Brock here needs to get back down to Earth."

Arielle smiled. "I could fly you across with my Ledyba if you'd like."

Ash was hoping Arielle would make that offer. The Ledyba looked really amazing.

"We can take you over one at a time," Arielle said. She blew her whistle, and the Ledyba hovered in the air. Arielle sat in the swing.

Ash didn't hesitate. He and Pikachu jumped into the swing next to Arielle.

Arielle blew the whistle again, and the Ledyba flew straight up. Ash felt air rushing around them as they flew over the river.

"What do you think, Pikachu?" Ash asked. "This is pretty cool, isn't it?"

Pikachu nodded happily. *"Pika!"*

Ledyba At Work

After two more trips, Misty and Brock were both across the river, too.

"Thanks a lot, Arielle," Ash said. "That was really great."

"No problem," Arielle said. "We had to come over here to work in this apple orchard, anyway."

Ash had been so excited to see the Ledyba that he didn't even notice the field of trees in front of them. Pretty white blossoms bloomed on the tree branches.

"What do the Ledyba do in an apple orchard?" Brock wondered.

"If you stay a while, I'll show you," Arielle said. She blew a short blast on her whistle, and the Ledyba formed two rows in front of her. Pikachu jumped on Ash's shoulder to get a better view.

"The wind is southwest at one knot," Arielle told the Ledyba. "Begin climbing at forty degrees when I blow the whistle."

Ash wasn't sure what Arielle was saying. Her words sounded like commands an airplane pilot might use.

Arielle blew the whistle, and the Ledyba flew up into the air. They hovered just above the trees.

Arielle blew the whistle again. "Descend!" she called out.

The Ledyba dropped down, and their feet touched the blossoms in the trees.

"Now climb!" Arielle called again. The Ledyba floated straight up again.

Arielle asked the Ledyba to climb and descend again and again. The Bug-type Pokémon moved from tree to tree.

"I see," Brock said. "The Ledyba are pollinating the orchard."

"I'm glad *you* see it," Ash said. "Now maybe you can explain it to me."

"It's simple," Brock said. "The Ledyba transfer pollen from apple blossom to apple blossom. That allows the trees to produce fruit."

"That's amazing," Misty said. "Arielle sure knows how to command her Ledyba."

Ash was impressed, too. Arielle blew the whistle one last time, then gave the Ledyba a rest. Ash approached her.

"So how did you learn to command your Ledyba like that?" he asked. Maybe he could pick up a trick or two.

Arielle held up the silver whistle. "I've done a lot of

training, but this whistle is the key. The Ledyba obey my commands when I play different notes on it. It's been passed down in my family for generations."

"Did someone say generations?" said a voice. "Then this is an antique!"

A strange-looking man walked up to the apple orchard. He wore a bow tie, a rumpled suit, and wire-rimmed eyeglasses. Behind him was a man in a tuxedo.

"Welcome to this special orchard edition of the Antiques Supershow," said the man in the tuxedo, talking into a microphone.

"Let's get down to business, shall we?" asked the man wearing the glasses. He grabbed the whistle and examined it with a magnifying glass. "Yes, yes, this is a wonderful antique. I give this whistle five stars." He stuck the whistle in his pocket.

"Bye-bye everybody, thanks for watching!" said the other man. The two began to walk away quickly.

"Hey, you can't take my whistle!" Arielle called out.

Ash tried to stop them, but things were happening too fast. In the blink of an eye, the two men tore off their costumes to reveal white uniforms underneath. One of them turned out to be a girl with long red hair. The other was a purple-haired boy.

"Team Rocket!" Ash cried.

A balloon with a Meowth face on it dropped down from the sky. Jessie and James jumped into the balloon basket and joined their Pokémon, Meowth.

Jessie laughed. "You won't be blowing the whistle on us this time," she said.

"That's right," said James. "Instead, we'll blow the whistle and steal your Ledyba!"

Jessie blew into the whistle, and a screeching sound filled the air.

Ash waited for the Ledyba to fly off, but the Bug-type Pokémon did not move. They sat on the ground and stared blankly at Jessie.

"What's wrong with you?" Jessie yelled at the Ledyba. "You're really starting to *bug* me, you know."

"The Ledyba won't obey you if you haven't done any training with them," Arielle snapped at her.

"Even though we blew the whistle," James said glumly, "I guess we blew it."

"This is a big bug rip-off!" screamed Meowth.

Ash stepped forward. "Don't talk to us about rip-offs. You're the thieves. Give us back Arielle's whistle!"

Jessie glared at Ash. "I'll give you twerps something. Go, Lickitung!"

Jessie threw out a red-and-white Poké Ball. A light flashed, and a pink Pokémon appeared on the rim of the balloon basket. Lickitung had a chunky body, a big, thick tail, and a long, sticky tongue.

"Lickitung, use Supersonic attack!" Jessie cried.

Lickitung opened its mouth, and waves of sonic energy pulsated from the Pokémon. Ash held his ears, and saw his friends do the same. He knew from experience that sonic waves could make you feel woozy.

Arielle turned to the Ledyba. "Use Tackle attack now!"

But the Ledyba couldn't move. Ash thought they looked sick.

"Those bugs won't budge," Meowth said. "I say we grab Pikachu!"

"That's what you think," Ash said. "Go, Pikachu. Use Thunderbolt attack now!"

Pikachu jumped down to the ground. A bolt of electric energy flew from Pikachu's body. The Thunderbolt hit the balloon, blasting a hole in it.

The balloon went spiraling across the sky. "Looks like Team Rocket's blasting off for the second time today!" they cried.

Ash started to cheer, but the look on Arielle's face stopped him. He followed her gaze.

The Ledyba were flying away.

"Oh, no!" Arielle cried. "Ledyba, come back!"

3

Follow the Ledyba Trail

"I'm sorry, Arielle," Ash said. "I didn't know Pikachu's Thunderbolt would scare away the Ledyba."

"You had no choice," Arielle said. "You had to do something to stop Team Rocket."

"It's too bad they got the whistle," Misty added.

Brock stepped in front of Arielle. "Don't worry. I'll find your Ledyba," he said confidently.

Brock held out a Poké Ball. "Go, Zubat!"

A Pokémon flew out of the ball and landed on Brock's shoulder. Zubat had a small body, leathery blue-and-purple wings, and pointy ears.

"Why Zubat?" Ash asked.

"Ledyba and Zubat both use Supersonic waves," Brock explained. "If Zubat's waves connect with the Ledyba's waves, we'll be able to track them down."

"Good idea!" Misty said.

"Zubat, use Supersonic to track down those Ledyba," Brock told his Pokémon. Zubat flew toward the trees and disappeared behind their leafy branches.

Soon the sound of flapping wings filled the air.

"It sounds like Zubat found them already," Brock said proudly.

But it wasn't Ledyba that came flying toward them. Instead, a large group of Golbat flapped and dipped through the trees. The evolved form of Zubat, each Golbat had a huge mouth filled with sharp fangs.

Brock quickly held out Zubat's Poké Ball. "Zubat, return!"

Zubat disappeared inside the ball. Without Zubat's Supersonic energy calling them, the Golbat flew back to the trees.

Brock looked sheepishly at Arielle. "Sorry," he said. "I was just trying to help, but I guess I got a little batty."

"That's all right," Arielle said. "Maybe we can find them some other way. My Ledyba love the smell of flowers. They might be in a garden somewhere."

"Hey, I have an idea," Ash said. He threw out a Poké Ball, and Heracross appeared. The Bug-type Pokémon was almost as tall as Ash. Heracross's tough skin was grayish-black, and it had a long horn that curved up over its head.

"Heracross, use your sniffer to take us to the nearest place that smells like flowers," Ash said.

Heracross sniffed the air. Then it began to slowly fly ahead of them.

"Let's follow it!" Ash suggested.

Heracross definitely seemed to be on the scent of something. It stopped at a large tree. Then it hugged the trunk with its legs and began to suck the sap from the tree.

Ash grimaced. Heracross was a great Pokémon, but sometimes all it could think about was eating tree sap.

"Sorry about that," Ash apologized. "I guess Heracross was more interested in sap than flowers." He returned Heracross to its Poké Ball.

Arielle smiled, but she still looked worried. "It's all right. I appreciate your help."

"Let's keep walking," Misty suggested. "We'll find them. I'm sure they didn't go far."

Arielle sighed. "Even if we do find them, I don't know if they'll listen to me. Without that whistle they won't do a thing I say."

They continued on through the orchard. After a while, the trees began to thin out.

"Ledyba! Where are you, Ledyba?" Brock called out.

Arielle stopped. "Do you guys smell that?"

Ash didn't smell anything.

"The Ledyba release a scented powder when they're in danger," Arielle explained. "I've been around them long enough to recognize the smell."

"That must mean they're nearby," Brock guessed.

Ash turned to Pikachu. "See if you can find them."

Pikachu ran to the nearest tree. It climbed up the tree by jumping from branch to branch.

"*Pika!*" it yelled excitedly. Ash looked up.

Pikachu was pointing at something.

"Let's go!" Ash said. Pikachu jumped down from the tree and ran ahead of them.

As they ran, Ash noticed a faint orange powder floating in the air.

"That's the powder that the Ledyba release," Arielle said. "We must be getting close."

They followed the powder through a grove of trees. They walked into a small clearing with a large tree in the center. Ash stopped in his tracks.

Jessie, James, and Meowth were sprawled on the grass, looking dazed. Meowth wore the silver whistle around its neck. Jessie's Cobra Pokémon, Arbok, had its long, purple body wrapped around the tree. Six ropes were tied to the end of Arbok's tail. At the end of each rope was one of Arielle's Ledyba!

Jessie stood up, smoothing out her white skirt. She glared at Arielle. "Those Ledyba of yours put up a good fight. But they're ours now!"

"You give back those Ledyba right now!" Ash yelled.

James jumped to his feet. He picked up a long tube off the ground and aimed it at Ash and the others.

"This'll teach you to *tangle* with us," James said. He pressed a button on the tube, and a large net flew out.

The net swooped over Ash, Arielle, Brock, Misty, and Pikachu, trapping them in a mess of knotted string.

"Hey!" Ash shouted.

"Now that we've got your attention," Jessie said, "why don't you hand over that Pikachu now!"

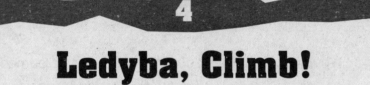

Ledyba, Climb!

"I would never, ever give Pikachu to you!" Ash shot back.

Jessie and James each held up a Poké Ball.

"We thought you might say that," Jessie said. "Lickitung, go!"

"Victreebel, too!" yelled James.

Lickitung popped out of Jessie's Poké Ball. Out of James's Poké Ball came Victreebel, a combination Grass- and Poison-type Pokémon. Victreebel's body was a large yellow flower bell.

The first thing Victreebel did was swallow James in one gulp.

"Why are you always doing this?" James screamed from inside the flower bulb. "Don't attack me. Go get that Pikachu!"

Victreebel spit out James. It hopped over to the net that held Ash and the others. Lickitung stomped alongside it.

Lickitung and Arbok's attack was harsh and clumsy. Lickitung jumped up and down on the net. Victreebel slammed its body into the huddled captives. Ash hugged Pikachu tightly to him.

"We need some help!" Misty cried.

Ash knew some of his Pokémon might be able to help them, but he couldn't reach his Poké Balls. He was too tangled up.

"My Ledyba might be able to help us," Arielle said. "But I don't know if they'll listen to me without my whistle."

"You can do it," Ash said. "You've spent so much time training them."

Arielle nodded. "Ledyba!" she yelled as loud as she could.

The Ledyba frantically flapped their wings at the sound of Arielle's voice. But the ropes kept them anchored to Arbok's tail.

"You can do it, Ledyba!" Arielle cheered. The Ledyba's wings buzzed even harder. Together, the six Ledyba yanked Arbok off the tree trunk. They flew toward the net with Arbok dangling upside down from the ropes.

Slam! The Ledyba used Arbok like a baseball bat and smacked into Lickitung and Victreebel.

The Pokémon landed in a stunned heap on the ground.

"Good work, Ledyba!" Arielle called out.

Without Lickitung on top of him, Ash was able to reach for a Poké Ball. He held it outside the net, and Bulbasaur, a blue-green Pokémon, appeared. A plant bulb grew on top of Bulbasaur's back.

"Bulbasaur, use your Razor Leaf attack to get us out of here," Ash said.

"Bulbasaur," said the Grass-type Pokémon. Sharp green leaves flew out of Bulbasaur's plant bulb. The leaves sliced through the net like knives. Ash and the others began to quickly untangle themselves from the strings.

"Victreebel, use your Razor Leaf attack, too!" James cried.

Victreebel was still angry from the Ledyba's attack. It turned its attention to the Bug-type Pokémon. Arbok

still dangled on the ropes attached to their bodies.

Sharp green leaves began to fly from Victreebel's mouth. Arielle noticed just in time.

"Ledyba, climb!" Arielle shouted.

The six Ledyba flew straight up in the air. The leaves missed hitting them. Instead, they sliced through the ropes, freeing them from Arbok.

Victreebel aimed another Razor Leaf attack at the Ledyba.

"Ledyba, descend!" Arielle yelled.

The six Ledyba dropped closer to the ground. The leaves flew harmlessly over their heads.

Jessie was angry. "Don't just stand there, Lickitung. Attack with Supersonic!"

Ash knew the Ledyba couldn't withstand another Supersonic attack.

"That won't work this time," Ash said. "Pikachu, use Thunderbolt now!"

Sparks sizzled on Pikachu's cheeks as it charged for the attack.

"Pikachuuuuuu!" A jagged bolt of electricity shot from Pikachu, striking Lickitung with full force. The blast sent Lickitung reeling into Jessie, James, Meowth, Victreebel, and Arbok. Team Rocket tumbled to the ground. The whistle flew out of Jessie's hands and landed at Arielle's feet.

"Ledyba, it's time for a Tackle attack. Full speed!" Arielle called out.

The Ledyba were happy to obey. All six Ledyba slammed into Team Rocket and their Pokémon. The collision sent the villains shooting through the sky.

"Looks like Team Rocket's buzzing off again!" they cried.

Arielle picked up the whistle. Then she ran to the Ledyba, who had landed on the grass. She hugged them one by one.

"I'm so glad you're back," she said. She turned to

Ash and his friends. "Thank you for your help."

"You're a great Trainer, Arielle," Misty said. "We'd all be in trouble if you hadn't handled those Ledyba so well."

Arielle looked at the whistle in her hand. "I guess maybe I didn't need this after all," she said.

Brock nodded. "It just goes to show that if you always treat your Pokémon with care, they'll always care about you, too."

Pikachu jumped into Ash's arms. "You can say that again!" Ash said.

5

Follow the Flying Hoppip

"It's a good thing we ran into Arielle and her Ledyba," Brock said the next day. Ash and his friends were walking through a grassy field, headed toward the next town. "Maybe we'll meet someone else we can help out." He had a dreamy look in his eyes.

Misty snorted. "Sure, Arielle needed our help, but she helped us out, too."

"And those Ledyba of hers were tough," Ash reminded him.

Misty stopped. "Look!"

Ash gazed around the field. Three Vileplume napped in a sunny spot. Each Pokémon had a short, squat body and a big red flower on top of its head. Nearby, three Bellsprout walked along on their plant-stem bodies. Each had a yellow flower bell for a head that bobbed up and down.

"There sure are a lot of Grass-type Pokémon living around here," Brock remarked.

Ash started to reply, but a strange sight stopped him. A small Pokémon hopped down the path toward them. The Pokémon had a round, pink body. Two jagged green leaves stuck out from the top of its head. It had orange eyes, big ears, a friendly smile, and it hopped along on two short legs.

"I think it's called a Hoppip," Brock said. "I can see why," Ash said. He took out Dexter.

"Hoppip, the Cottonweed Pokémon," said the computer. "This Pokémon is light as a feather and can be lifted by the gentlest breeze."

Just as Dexter finished, a breeze started to blow. And just as Dexter had described, the breeze picked up the Hoppip. It carried the Hoppip away from them.

"We can't let it blow away!" Misty cried. She took off

after the Hoppip.

"Wait up!" Ash called out. He, Brock, and Pikachu ran after them.

Ash and the others followed the Hoppip down a dirt path. They turned a corner, and a girl stood there. She had blue hair, and the pink scarf around her neck matched her pants. The girl held a long stick with a net attached to one end.

She looked startled to see them. Then she composed herself and expertly scooped up the Hoppip in the net. Ash noticed a group of Hoppip at her feet.

The girl smiled. "You guys surprised me," she said. "I'm Mariah."

"I'm Ash, and these are my friends Brock, Misty, and Pikachu," Ash said. "Sorry we surprised you. We were trying to help that Hoppip. Are those all wild Hoppip, or do they belong to you?"

"They're mine," Mariah said. "Why don't you follow me? You look like you've been walking for a while."

"I'd follow you anywhere," Brock said. He had that goofy look in his eyes that he always got when he was

around an interesting girl.

Ash and his friends followed Mariah a short distance to a log cabin. Next to the cabin was a large area surrounded by netting on all sides. Mariah lifted up the net and invited them to step inside. Seven Hoppip hopped in ahead of them.

Ash looked back at the cabin. Strange instruments were attached to the roof. Metal cups attached to silver rods twirled around in the light breeze.

"You must do a lot more than just train Hoppip, Mariah," Ash said. "What is all that stuff up there?"

"I'm a weather forecaster," Mariah explained. "Those instruments help me make predictions about the weather. The Hoppip help me do that, too."

Ash couldn't believe it. "How?"

Mariah nodded toward the Hoppip. "Watch."

The Hoppip had been wandering around the enclosure. Now they began to group together.

"The wind is going to pick up any second," Mariah said. "The Hoppip always cluster together like that before a breeze."

Sure enough, Ash felt a cool breeze on his arms. The breeze lifted two Hoppip off the ground. The

Pokémon hit the net, and then gently floated to the ground.

"That breeze would only rate a two on the Hoppip scale," Mariah said. "That means it's only strong enough to pick up two Hoppip."

"Wow," Ash said, impressed.

Brock pointed. "Hey, they're all grouping together again."

Ash felt another wind blow up, this one a little stronger than before. This time, all seven Hoppip were lifted up into the air. They swirled around the enclosure, but they were safe inside the net. Ash knew they wouldn't be carried away.

Suddenly, another Hoppip ran past them. Ash was puzzled. He was sure there were only seven Hoppip. Where had this one come from?

The new Hoppip climbed on top of a rock. It jumped off, but the wind didn't carry it like it did the others. This one landed with a thump on the grass.

"Poor little thing," Misty said. She ran to the Hoppip's side.

"Is there something wrong with that one?" Ash asked.

Mariah smiled. "You could say that one's a little

different from the others."

Misty took a bandanna from her pocket and patted the Hoppip. "Let me clean you up a little bit," she said sweetly.

As Misty wiped the Hoppip, Ash saw that a pink powder was coming off. This Pokémon wasn't pink at all, like the other Hoppip. Its body was dark blue.

Ash gasped. "Hey, that's not a Hoppip," he said. "That's an Oddish!"

6

Tornado!

"I know it seems strange," Mariah said. "This Oddish lives in the neighborhood. It spends so much time playing with my Hoppip that it wishes it were a Hoppip, too."

As she spoke, Oddish climbed up on a wooden fence. It jumped off. This time it landed in a haystack.

Mariah sighed. "I've tried to tell it that it's an Oddish, but it's determined to fly like the Hoppip," she explained.

Misty helped the Oddish get back on its feet. The little Pokémon looked sad.

"I think you're a great Pokémon even if you don't know how to fly," Misty said.

Still, the Oddish looked sad. Ash felt sorry for it. He thought Oddish was a cool Pokémon. He didn't like to see it feeling bad about itself.

Another breeze kicked up, and this one felt stronger than before. Ash noticed that Mariah was concerned. The Hoppip were all back on the ground, and they were forming another group. The leaves on top of each Hoppip's head were pressed together.

Mariah's concerned expression changed to one of alarm. "Oh, no!" she cried. "There's a huge windstorm on the way."

"How do you know it's going to be big?" Brock asked.

Mariah pointed to the Hoppip's leaves. "Hoppip only put their leaves together like that before extremely strong winds. It's very rare. We've got to get inside!"

The sky grew dark as Ash and his friends helped Mariah round up the Hoppip and Oddish and bring them inside the log cabin. More weather machines filled the inside of the cabin, as well as a large computer.

Mariah grabbed a notebook and a pen and began to take readings from the machines.

"All of my instruments confirm what my Hoppip already told me," Mariah said. "There's a tornado headed this way!"

Ash looked out the window. Angry looking black clouds were quickly gathering in the sky. A strong wind was blowing away everything that wasn't anchored down.

"What can we do?" Ash asked.

"Let's start by boarding the windows," Mariah said. They all helped hammer wooden boards over every window in the room. Outside, the roar of the winds grew louder. The Hoppip and the Oddish huddled together in the center of the room.

"Let's all take cover under my desk," Mariah called out over the roaring winds. "It's the safest place."

Ash picked up Pikachu and headed for the desk. Suddenly, the whole cabin began to shake violently. Ash heard a terrible groan from above. He looked up. The wind was tearing the roof off of the cabin.

To his horror, Ash saw that the wind had picked up the Hoppip. They began to rise up toward the open roof.

"No! My Hoppip!" Mariah yelled. She ran toward the center of the room with her arms outstretched. Ash knew the strong winds could easily pick her up.

Brock rushed to her rescue. "I've got you, Mariah!"

he yelled. He grabbed her around the waist and pulled her underneath the desk. Mariah looked devastated as the Hoppip disappeared through the roof.

Next, the tornado picked up Oddish. Misty jumped out from under the desk.

"Oddish, grab on!" she shouted. But the winds carried Oddish out of her reach.

Now Misty was in danger, too.

"Misty!" Ash yelled. He made sure Pikachu was safe. Then he jumped out and grabbed onto Misty's legs just as the tornado was about to carry her away.

They struggled to crawl back to safety.

"What do we do now?" Ash called to Mariah.

"We wait until the storm passes," Mariah called back. She looked up at the dark sky. "There's nothing to do but wait and hope."

7

A Hoppip Rescue
Mission

The storm passed as quickly as it came. Ash and the others stayed under the desk until they were sure it was safe. Then the inside of the cabin was filled with sunshine. Ash looked out from under the desk. The sky above them was clear blue.

Ash and Pikachu stepped out into the room. Splintered wood and debris covered the floor.

Mariah, Brock, and Misty emerged from under the desk. Everyone seemed to be okay.

"We're a lot luckier than your house was, Mariah,"

Ash remarked.

Misty frowned. *"We're* lucky, but I wonder if the Oddish and the Hoppip are."

"We've got to look for them," Ash said.

Mariah managed a smile. "Thanks for volunteering to help," she said. "Let's go find them!"

They stepped outside. The net around the enclosed area had collapsed. Not far away, the roof had landed in the middle of a field. Ash and the others ran to it.

"At least it didn't land on anybody," Mariah said, after checking underneath.

A tiny whimper followed Mariah's words. Pikachu's ears twitched as it followed the noise. *"Pikachu!"* Pikachu ran a few feet away, where two little blue legs were sticking up in the air.

"It's Oddish!" Misty cried.

Mariah picked it up. The Pokémon looked dazed, but not hurt.

"Oddish! Oddish! Oddish!" The Pokémon chattered away. The leaves on top of its head waved excitedly.

"Oddish wants to start looking for its Hoppip friends right away," Mariah explained.

Oddish jumped out of Mariah's arms. It stood still

for a moment. Then its leaves began to wiggle.

"Oddish! Oddish!" it cried. Then it hopped away toward the woods.

Ash and the others followed Oddish. The Pokémon stopped at the base of a tree.

"Oddish! Oddish!" Oddish jumped up and down.

Ash looked up. A Hoppip was stuck in the crook of a tree branch.

"Good work, Oddish," Mariah said, patting its head. "Now we just have to get it down."

"I'll do it, Mariah," Brock said quickly. He climbed up the tree and returned with the Hoppip in his arms.

"Thanks, Brock," Mariah said. She looked down at Oddish. "Now we only have six more to find."

"Oddish!" The Grass-type Pokémon's leaves began to wiggle again. Oddish hopped off through the woods.

This time it led them to a stream. A Hoppip was holding on to a tree branch that was stuck in the water.

"If we don't move fast, it'll get washed away!" Misty cried.

Ash tried to think of a way to rescue it, but Brock jumped in the water before he could make a move.

Soon Brock was back at Mariah's side, handing her another Hoppip.

"Brock, you're the best!" Mariah said.

Brock's cheeks turned red.

"Oddish! Oddish!" Now the little Pokémon was jumping up and down like crazy.

"What is it?" Mariah asked.

Ash knew the answer. Floating toward them was a hot-air balloon with a Meowth face. Inside the balloon basket was Team Rocket – and the five lost Hoppip!

"What are those Pokémon thieves up to now?" Ash wondered.

"Pokémon thieves?" Mariah looked angry. "Give me back my Hoppip!" she called up to them.

Meowth laughed. "These Hoppip are ours now!"

Misty stepped forward, holding a Poké Ball. "We'll see about that. Staryu, I choose you!"

A star-shaped Pokémon burst from the Poké Ball. Staryu zipped through the air, tearing into the balloon with its five points. The balloon burst with a bang, and then crashed into the grass.

Jessie frowned. "That Staryu certainly does have a point," she said.

"Give us back those Hoppip!" Ash yelled.

"Not without a fight," said James. "Victreebel, go!"

James's Pokémon came out of its ball and promptly swallowed James.

"Go after them, not me!" James complained.

Victreebel spit out James and faced Ash, who was already throwing a Poké Ball in the air.

"Go Heracross!" Ash cried.

The big Bug-type Pokémon flew out of the ball and lined up next to Staryu. Jessie threw out Arbok, and the purple Pokémon lined up next to Victreebel. The two teams of Pokémon faced each other. A battle was about to begin.

And then Oddish hopped right in the middle.

"Oddish, what are you doing?" Mariah cried.

"I think Oddish wants to battle," Misty said.

James laughed. "I think my Victreebel is finally going to have a *victory*. Victreebel, Tackle attack now!"

But Oddish didn't give Victreebel a chance to make a move. Oddish delivered two strong kicks to Victreebel that knocked the Pokémon on its back. Ash was impressed by the power of Oddish's kick.

Misty noticed it, too. "Oddish has a super-strong kick. It must be from all that hopping," she guessed.

Victreebel tried to get up, but Oddish wiggled its leaves, and tiny grains of gold floated out. The gold dust covered Victreebel. The Pokémon became as still as a stone, and then collapsed once more.

"And Oddish is the winner!" Ash cried.

"Not yet," Jessie said. "Arbok, try a Bite attack!"

"Arbok!" Jessie's Pokémon lunged at Oddish. The Grass-type Pokémon hopped straight up in the air. It shot a mist of white crystal powder at Arbok.

"Wow," Misty remarked, "it's almost like it can fly!"

Arbok's eyes began to close. Soon the Pokémon was snoring.

"Oddish used Sleep Powder," Brock said.

Meowth leaped in front of Arbok. "This is getting embarrassing," it said. "It's Slash attack time!" Sharp claws popped out of Meowth's paws.

Oddish didn't even flinch. A powerful beam of yellow sunlight poured out of its head. The beam grew stronger as it got closer to Team Rocket.

Bam! The Solar Beam slammed into Jessie, James, Meowth, Arbok, and Victreebel, sending them flying across the sky.

"Looks like Team Rocket's flying away again!" they cried.

The five Hoppip hopped out of the fallen balloon basket and surrounded Oddish.

"Oddish! Oddish!" The Pokémon cheered and jumped up happily.

Mariah hugged Oddish. The other Hoppip jumped into her arms.

"I can't tell you how happy I am that you're all safe," Mariah said.

"And it's all because of Oddish," said Misty.

"Oddish?" The little Pokémon looked like it didn't believe her.

Ash nodded. "Any Pokémon that battles as hard as you do has a lot to be proud of, even if it can't float on the wind," he said.

"Pokémon are all different, and they're all good at different things," Brock added. "Nobody's good at everything. Just remember — it's what you *can* do, not what you *can't* do, that counts."

Mariah looked into Oddish's eyes. "From now on we'll think of you as an honorary Hoppip that's a little 'oddish.' How about that?"

Oddish smiled and hopped up and down.

"Oddish!" it said happily.

8

What's a Wooper?

A few days had passed since they left Mariah and the Hoppip, and Brock couldn't stop talking about their encounter.

"Remember how I saved all those Hoppip?" Brock said. He sighed dreamily. "I did it all for Mariah."

Misty rolled her eyes. "You helped, Brock," she admitted. "But that Oddish really saved the day."

"Misty's right," Ash said. "Oddish was awesome."

The friends continued to walk along a mountain road. Ash knew there was a town coming up soon, but he wasn't sure when they'd get there.

He didn't have long to wait. Soon the mountain road

ended on top of a hill. The hill sloped down sharply, leading to a small village below. A circle of small houses sat in the front of the village. There was a pond in the center of the circle, and each house had a pink, dome-shaped roof.

"I wonder what kind of buildings those are," Misty said.

Brock looked thoughtful. "Hmm. From the looks of them, I'd say – whoa! There's something cold and slimy on my back!"

Ash watched as his friend wriggled around, trying to shake something off of his back. Then Brock lost his footing and went tumbling down the hill.

"Brock!" Ash yelled. He, Misty, and Pikachu climbed down the hill after him.

They found Brock sprawled in the grass. A girl with black hair tied in two pigtails stood over him. In her arms she held a strange-looking Pokémon. Its round head was the largest part of its body. The Pokémon had two ears that looked like tree branches sticking out of the side of its head, and a flat tail. Its slick, blue skin was the same light-blue color as the girl's T-shirt, and it had a black marking shaped like a heart on its belly.

"My name's Olesia," said the girl. "This is my Wooper. I hope it didn't cause you any trouble."

Brock quickly rose to his feet. "Trouble? No trouble at all. I'm Brock."

Misty cleared her throat. "And we're Misty and Ash."

Ash was curious about the Pokémon. "What's a Wooper?" he asked. He took out Dexter.

"Wooper, the Water Fish Pokémon, evolves into Quagsire." said the computer. "Living in cold water, these Pokémon forage for food on land in cool weather. When on land, Wooper is protected by a liquid membrane."

Brock grimaced. "I guess that's why Wooper felt so slimy on my back."

Olesia smiled. "You get used to it. I know I have. I run a preschool for Wooper." She motioned an arm at the pink-roofed buildings.

"That explains why the houses look so cute," Misty said.

Olesia nodded. "The Wooper like it here. The water in this pond is perfect for raising them."

At mention of the pond, Olesia's Wooper walked over and jumped in. Ash saw that there were about a dozen other Wooper swimming around. He noticed these Wooper didn't have a heart marking, instead, they had three horizontal lines on their bellies.

The Wooper played and splashed in the water. Pikachu leaned over the pond, watching the Wooper. Misty placed Togepi on the shallow end of the pond. The little Pokémon kicked its tiny legs happily, splashing drops of water on Misty's face.

Misty giggled and picked up Togepi. "These

Wooper look like they're having fun," she said. "Would you mind showing us what you do here?"

"Of course not," Olesia said. She walked to one of the buildings and returned with a tambourine.

"Okay, everyone," she called to the Wooper. "It's playtime."

"Woop! Woop!" The Wooper smiled and lined up in the pond.

Olesia began to sing a pretty tune with no words. She jingled the tambourine.

"Wooper! Wooper! Wooper!" The little Water-type Pokémon sang along with the tune and swam in a circle.

"Oh, how cute!" Misty said, delighted. Ash had to admit they were pretty cute.

But he was even more impressed with the way Olesia handled them. They really listened to her. Ash knew from experience that it wasn't always easy for a Pokémon Trainer to get his or her Pokémon to obey.

The sound of a ringing phone interrupted Olesia's song. Olesia took a cell phone from her pocket and pressed a button. A disturbed look crossed her face.

"Don't worry, Mom," she said. "I'll be right there."

"What's the matter?" Misty asked.

"My mother lives in the next town, and she fell down the stairs," Olesia said. "The ambulance is on its way. She says she's all right, but I have to be certain."

Olesia's gaze drifted to the Wooper in the pond, and she bit her lip. "I can't just leave the Wooper here. I'm in a real bind."

Ash was about to offer to help when Brock stepped in front of him. "Don't worry. I, Brock, will help you."

"We'll all help you," Misty said. "Go see to your mother. We'll watch the Wooper."

Olesia looked relieved. "Thanks so much, guys. This is a big help."

Olesia led them to one of the buildings. She went inside and came out with a small notebook. She handed it to Brock.

"These are instructions for taking care of the Wooper," she told him.

"Got it," Brock said.

Olesia walked over to a motor scooter, strapped on a helmet, and rode off down the street.

Brock opened the notebook and began to read. Ash and Misty looked over his shoulder.

"Is it going to be hard taking care of these Wooper?" Misty asked.

"No worries," Brock said confidently. "Taking care of a few little Wooper is nothing for the future top Pokémon breeder in the world." Brock put down the book. "Let's go see the little guys."

Ash and Misty followed Brock around the building. There was the pond. But it was empty.

"*Pika!*" cried Pikachu.

Ash froze. "The Wooper," Ash said.

"They've all disappeared!" wailed Misty.

Follow that Wooper!

"Olesia will never forgive me," Brock moaned.

Ash tried to console his friend. "Don't worry," he said. "I'm sure we'll find them."

Pikachu was already looking for clues. The little yellow Pokémon circled the pond. It stopped at a puddle of water near the pond's edge.

"Pika!" Pikachu called to Ash.

Ash walked over and examined the puddle. A water trail led from the pond to the buildings of the nursery school.

"The Wooper must have left these tracks," Ash guessed. "Let's go!"

They followed the trail to the largest of the pink-roofed buildings. The water drops led right to the door.

"Great!" Brock opened the door.

An unbelievable scene greeted them. The Wooper were inside the kitchen, eating everything in sight. Every cabinet was open. Boxes of crackers and cookies were spilled all over the floor, along with all kinds of liquids.

"They must be hungry," Misty said.

"It's a good thing I read Olesia's book," Brock said. "Lesson One: Always show affection when interacting with Wooper."

Brock handed Olesia's notebook to Ash. Then he took off his backpack and reached inside. He took out a handful of the special Pokémon food he made. Brock held out his hand and offered the food to the Wooper.

"Here, little Wooper. I know you're hungry. Eat some of my food so you can grow big and strong," Brock said in a gentle voice.

One by one, the Wooper approached Brock. One Wooper took a bite of food from Brock's hand. *"Woop! Woop!"* it said happily.

The other Wooper swarmed over Brock, clamoring for the food. Ash couldn't even see his friend. Brock was covered with at least a dozen excited Wooper.

"Help!" Brock cried. He shook his arms and legs, sending the Wooper flying off him.

"You're going to have to do better than that if you're going to be the world's top Pokémon breeder," Misty teased.

Brock blushed. "For a minute there, I thought I was going to be Wooper food!"

Ash looked in Olesia's notebook. "Lesson Two: Use a tambourine when instructing Wooper," he read.

Misty found an extra tambourine hanging on the

kitchen wall. "Leave it to me."

Misty put Togepi on the ground and began to shake the tambourine. *"Changa changa changa,"* she sang.

Ash grimaced. Misty's music sounded different than Olesia's. For one thing, it was a lot worse.

The Wooper thought so, too. Their stick-like ears folded over so they couldn't hear her.

Misty noticed the unhappy Wooper and frowned. "What did I do wrong?" she asked.

"Togi! Togi!" Togepi waved its arms.

"Do you want to try?" Misty asked. She handed the tambourine to Togepi.

The little Pokémon hopped from leg to leg, shaking the tambourine. The Wooper smiled.

"Wooper! Wooper!" they sang along.

Togepi started to walk back to the pond. The Wooper followed it, forming a line. Soon the Wooper were back in the pond where they belonged.

"Good work, Togepi," Brock said. "What a relief!"

"Don't be too relieved yet," said Misty. "I think we're missing one. Where's Olesia's Wooper?"

Ash examined the Wooper in the pond. Misty was

right. Olesia's Wooper, with the heart-shaped mark, was nowhere in sight.

"We'll find it," Ash said. "Misty, Pikachu, and I will go look for it. Brock, stay here and make sure these Wooper don't go anywhere."

"And take care of Togepi, too," Misty added.

Brock settled down at the pond's edge. Togepi continued to dance and play the tambourine. The Wooper in the pond looked happy, but poor Brock looked devastated. He didn't want to disappoint Olesia.

"Maybe it's back in the kitchen," Ash suggested. They walked back to the cabin. Sure enough, Olesia's Wooper sat in the sink on top of a pile of dirty dishes.

"Stay there, Wooper," Ash said. He leaned over with his arms outstretched.

"Woop!" The Wooper jumped out of the sink and onto a pile of dishes stacked high on the counter.

"Wait!" Ash cried.

The Wooper jumped again, jarring two dishes from the pile. Ash dived and caught the dishes. He landed face down on the floor.

"Woop!" Wooper jumped on Ash's head and landed back on the counter. It zoomed down the counter toward the open door.

"Pika!" Pikachu ran on the floor, keeping pace with the Wooper above it.

"Woop!" The Wooper knocked over a bowl of silverware. Forks and spoons clattered on top of Pikachu's head, stopping the Pokémon in its tracks.

Ash struggled to get to his feet, Misty ran to help Pikachu, and the Wooper scooted right out the door.

Pikachu was the first one after it.

"Follow that Wooper!" Ash called.

Ash and Misty followed Pikachu down the road that led out of town. Pikachu stopped at the bottom of the steep hill. There was the Wooper, smiling down at them.

"How did it get up there?" Misty wondered.

"There isn't time to worry about that now," Ash said. He hoisted Pikachu on his back and began climbing to the top. Misty joined him.

By the time they reached the top, Wooper was already hurrying down the trail. Wooper stopped at a wooden bridge. The bridge crossed a narrow gorge. Ash saw that a river flowed far below − a long way down.

Narrow planks of wood were tied together to form the bridge, and thin ropes acted as handrails. The bridge swayed in the breeze. It didn't look like anyone had crossed it in a long time.

"Hey, Wooper. Come on over here," Ash called out.

"Woop!" Wooper hopped over the wooden planks and stopped in the middle of the bridge.

Ash took a step onto the bridge. The wood creaked under his feet.

"Come back to me, Wooper," Ash said. But the Wooper didn't budge.

"Pika!" Pikachu began to crawl gingerly across the bridge. Ash got on his hands and knees and followed his Pokémon.

Misty hesitated at first. But then the Wooper hopped on top of the rope railing and began running back and forth.

"Be careful, Wooper," Misty said. "You're going to fall." She got on her hands and knees and crawled alongside Ash.

Wooper ran back and forth along the railing. The bridge swayed and creaked.

"Woop!" Wooper jumped off the railing and landed safely on the other side.

"Thank goodness," Misty said.

But the bridge was creaking even louder now. Ash could see that the rope railing was dangerously frayed.

The bridge was going to fall apart any second.

"Hurry!" Ash cried.

Pikachu ran across the planks and jumped onto the grass. Ash felt the middle of the bridge begin to sag under his feet.

Snap! The bridge snapped in two. Ash grabbed on to a plank and held on as tightly as he could.

"Hold on, Misty!" he yelled.

A Slippery Catch

Ash closed his eyes. The half of the bridge he was holding on to swung to the other side of the gorge.

"Whoa!" Misty screamed next to him.

Now they were hanging down the side of the gorge. Ash opened his eyes. They could climb up the planks of the bridge like a ladder to get to the top.

"Pika?" Pikachu wanted to know if they were all right.

"We'll be up in a minute," Ash called to Pikachu. "Go get that Wooper!"

Side by side, Ash and Misty climbed up the planks of the bridge. The muscles in Ash's arms strained with each movement.

Finally, exhausted, they reached the top.

"Let's go," Ash said. "With any luck, Pikachu has found Wooper by now."

The bridge led to a dirt trail, which seemed like their best bet. Ash and Misty followed the trail. Soon they heard voices, and the two friends broke into a run.

The trail of voices led to a disturbing scene. Olesia's Wooper was there, and Pikachu was standing in front of it. But facing them were Jessie, James, and Meowth. Jessie held a Poké Ball in one hand.

"Team Rocket!" Ash cried. "That Wooper already has a Trainer."

"You won't be able to catch it with a Poké Ball," Misty added.

James frowned. "But we've *got* to capture this Wooper."

"Why?" Ash asked.

"It's so cute," Meowth explained. "The Boss'll take one look at it and forgive us for screwing up so much."

"I think it'll take more than a Wooper to make up for that," Misty mumbled.

"Don't listen to those twerps," Jessie said. "There's more than one way to catch a Wooper!"

Jessie reached behind her back and pulled out two nets attached to long poles. She handed one to James.

"Pikachu, cover the Wooper," Ash said.

"Pika!" Pikachu picked up the Wooper.

"Woop!" The slippery Wooper slid out of Pikachu's grasp. Meowth grabbed it.

"Woop!" Wooper popped out of Meowth's arms. This time James grabbed it.

"Woop! Woop! Woop!" No one could get a grip on the slippery Wooper. One by one, James, Ash, and Misty tried to grab it, only to have it pop back out of their arms again.

While the others were struggling with the Wooper, Jessie threw out a Poké Ball.

"Go, Arbok!" Jessie shouted.

The purple Cobra Pokémon exploded from the ball in a flash of white light. Arbok jumped in between them, sending Wooper flying away. Wooper landed in a nearby patch of grass.

James threw a Poké Ball next. "Weezing, use Smoke Screen!"

There was a puff of smoke, and a Pokémon that looked like a toxic purple cloud appeared. Weezing had one large, round head with a smaller head attached to it.

Weezing launched right into its Smoke Screen attack. Clouds of thick, foul-smelling smoke poured from Weezing's body. The dark smoke quickly filled the air.

Ash coughed. His eyes burned. He couldn't see a thing.

Then a breeze kicked up, blowing away the smoke. Ash opened his eyes.

"Wooper!" Ash cried.

Team Rocket was back in their balloon. Jessie held a net in one hand, and Olesia's Wooper was trapped inside it!

11

Don't Mess
With Wooper!

"Now we can take this little cutie to the Boss," Meowth said.

"Not so fast!" cried an angry voice.

Ash turned. Olesia rode up on her motor scooter with Brock seated behind her.

Olesia stopped the bike and got off. "That's my Wooper!" she shouted. "What are you guys doing with it?"

Jessie grinned. "We're stealing it, of course," she said. "And now we must be going." The balloon rose up from the ground.

Brock reached for a Poké Ball. "We've got to get back Olesia's Wooper. Go, everybody!"

Olesia put a hand on his shoulder. "Wait, Brock," she said. "My Wooper will be fine."

Ash wasn't sure what Olesia was up to. He watched to see what she would do next.

"Wooper, playtime is over!" Olesia called up to the balloon. "It's time to go back now."

Wooper didn't hesitate. It hopped out of the net and landed on the edge of the balloon basket. One more hop, and it landed on the ground in front of Olesia.

"Don't let it get away, Arbok!" Jessie shrieked.

"You go, too, Weezing!" James barked. Arbok and Weezing flew out of the balloon. Olesia just smiled confidently.

"Lesson Three," said Olesia. "Don't mess with Wooper!"

She turned to her Wooper. "Use Tackle!"

"Woop!" Wooper jumped in the air. It slammed its little body into Arbok, and then Weezing. The two Pokémon fell to the ground, stunned.

Wooper wasn't finished. It used its flat tail to smack each Pokémon on the head.

"That's one strong Wooper," Brock remarked.

"Wooper, now use Slam!" Olesia yelled.

"Woop!" Wooper jumped up and bounced on Weezing's head. Then it used its tail to pick up Arbok. Weezing thrashed Arbok against the ground again and again.

"All right, Wooper. Now get them out of here," Olesia said.

"Woop!" Wooper began to twirl Arbok around and around in circles. Arbok banged into Weezing. Then Wooper sent Arbok and Weezing flying into the balloon.

"Nooooo!" cried Jessie, James, and Meowth.

Slam! Arbok and Weezing crashed into the balloon. The force sent Team Rocket sailing over the horizon.

"Looks like Team Rocket's blasting off again!" they cried.

"That was cool, Wooper," Misty said.

"Woop!" replied Wooper.

Olesia smiled. "My Wooper is stronger than you think."

Ash had to admit it was true. He thought about the other Pokémon they had met in the Johto Region. The Ledyba and Hoppip both looked really cute. But they were also really powerful.

Olesia and Wooper hopped on the motor scooter. "Follow me, guys," Olesia said. "Let's go back to the school and eat."

Brock got a goofy look at his face as Olesia rode away. "She's probably grateful to me for saving her Wooper."

Misty groaned. "Brock, you were the one who lost the Wooper in the first place. If it wasn't for Togepi and Pikachu, they'd still be running around."

Brock blushed. "I guess you're right."

"Don't be too hard on yourself, Brock,"

Ash said. "We helped out. But I think I'm learning something about Pokémon."

"What's that?" Misty asked.

"Never underestimate a Pokémon," Ash said. "Even cute Pokémon know how to take care of themselves."

"Pika!" agreed Pikachu.

Ash picked up Pikachu and headed off down the trail. So far, the Pokémon in the Johto Region were full of surprises.

He couldn't wait to see what would happen next!

About the Author

Tracey West has been writing books for more than twenty years. She enjoys watching cartoons, reading comic books, and taking long walks in the woods (looking for wild Pokémon). She lives in a small town in New York with her family and pets.

Next in this series:

Ash heads to Azalea Town to battle for the Hive Badge. But first he has to finish a top-secret mission for Professor Oak. The mysteries of the GS Ball are about to be revealed − or are they?

Along the way, Brock catches a new Pokémon and Team Rocket messes things up again. Then Ash finally faces off for his second Johto League badge. Will he squish Bugsy's swarm of Bug-type Pokémon? Or will he suffer the sting of defeat?